Andy Griffiths is one of Australia's funniest
and most successful authors. His books include
the extremely popular *Just!* series, which has sold
over two million copies worldwide, as well as the
New York Times bestselling Bum trilogy. He lives
in Melbourne with his wife, two daughters
and one (non-flat) cat.

Tenderised at an early age by his four brothers,
Terry Denton somehow survived childhood in inner
suburban Melbourne. He escaped to the seaside where he
started writing and illustrating children's books. He is best
known for his illustrations in Andy Griffiths' *Just!* series
and *The Bad Book*, and for his own *Gasp!* books and *Wombat
and Fox* stories. He shares a house with his wife and three
children and a lawn mower and an electric pencil sharpener
and a pop-up toaster that only toasts toast on one side.

ANDY GRIFFITHS

THE CAT ON THE MAT IS FLAT

ILLUSTRATED BY TERRY DENTON

Pan

Pan Macmillan Australia

First published 2006 in Pan by Pan Macmillan Australia Pty Limited
1 Market Street, Sydney

Reprinted 2007, 2008 (twice), 2010, 2011, 2012

National Library of Australia
Cataloguing-in-Publication data:

Griffiths, Andy, 1961– .
The cat on the mat is flat.

For primary school children.
ISBN 978 0 330 42260 4.

1. Humorous stories, Australian. 2. Children's stories, Australian.
I. Denton, Terry, 1950– . II. Title.
A823.3

Internal design by Liz Seymour and Terry Denton
Inside cover photograph of Andy Griffiths and Terry Denton
by James Penlidis
Typeset in 18/25 Janson Text
Printed in Australia by McPherson's Printing Group

Contents

THE CAT,
THE MAT,
THE RAT,
AND THE
BASEBALL BAT

The cat sat.
The cat sat on the mat.

The cat sat on the mat
and as it sat
it saw a rat.

The cat jumped up
and chased
the rat

around
and around
and around
the mat.

The rat did not like
being chased by the cat,
and after three laps
around the mat

the rat said,
'That's enough of that!'
And it went
and got ...

a baseball bat.

The rat
chased the cat.

The rat
chased the cat
with the
baseball bat.

Around
and around
and around
the mat

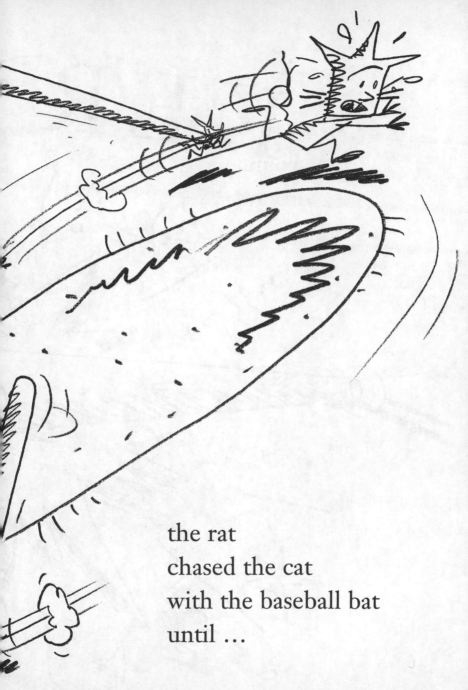

the rat
chased the cat
with the baseball bat
until ...

KER

SPLAT!

Never again
did that cat
chase the rat—
the cat
was much too flat
for that.

ED AND TED
AND
TED'S DOG
FRED

There was a man
whose name was Ed.

Ed lived in a shed
with his friend Ted.

Ted had a dog
whose name
was Fred.

Ed liked Ted
and Ted liked Ed

and Fred liked Ted
but he didn't like Ed.

One morning Fred
jumped on Ed's bed.

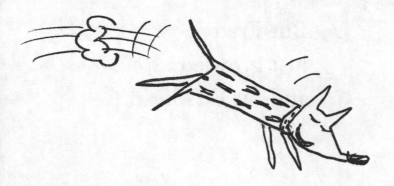

Ed said: 'Fred,
get off my bed!'

But Fred
just growled
and bit Ed's head.

Ed saw red
and then
he said:

'I'm fed up
with Fred
always biting
my head!

I'm leaving this shed.'

And he went
to his car
(which
was
red).

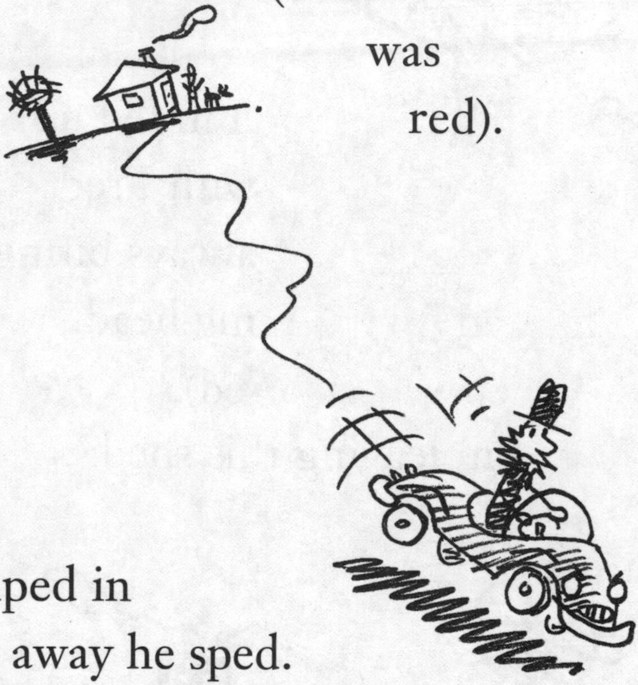

He
jumped in
and away he sped.

Ted said:
'Ed! Come back to the shed!'
But Ed just shook his head
and fled.

So Ted jumped in his car
(which was also red).

But it wouldn't start.
The battery was dead.

Ted stamped his feet
and his face went red.
'Bother! Bother! Bother!' he said.
'I'll have to take the sled instead.'

Ted hitched up Fred
to the front of the sled
(which, by the way,
was also red)
and away
from the shed
sped Fred and Ted.

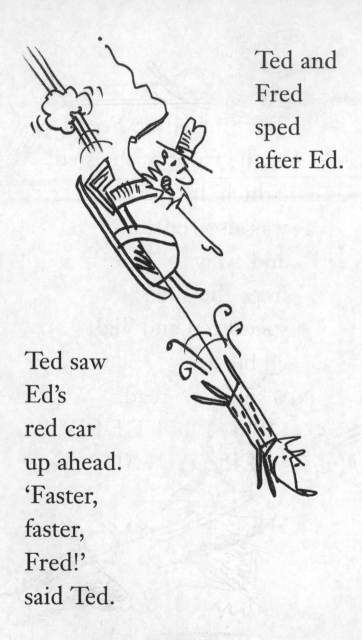

Ted and
Fred
sped
after Ed.

Ted saw
Ed's
red car
up ahead.
'Faster,
faster,
Fred!'
said Ted.

Ted and Fred
were gaining on Ed,
but all of a sudden,
Ed stopped dead.
There was
a road block
and a sign that read,
'STOP! DO NOT DRIVE!
BIG CLIFF AHEAD!'

Ted said, 'Fred!
Stop the sled!'
But Fred
could not.
On they sped!

Ted and Fred
smashed into Ed.

Over
the
cliff
Ed
plumm-et-ed!
Closely
followed
by
Ted
and
Fred.

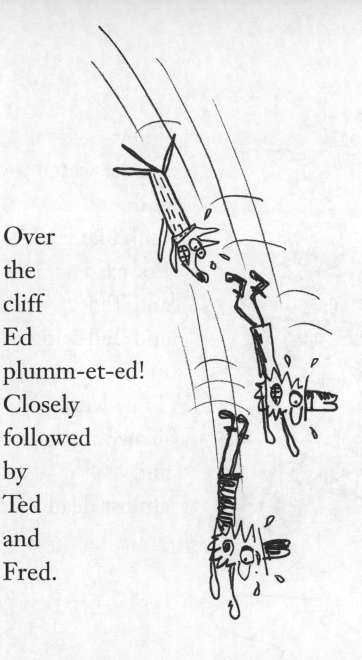

They
hit the water
and
sank like lead.
Poor Ed
and Ted
and Ted's dog
Fred!
They were
drowning
and
almost dead ...

when they were swallowed
by a whale
called
Ned.

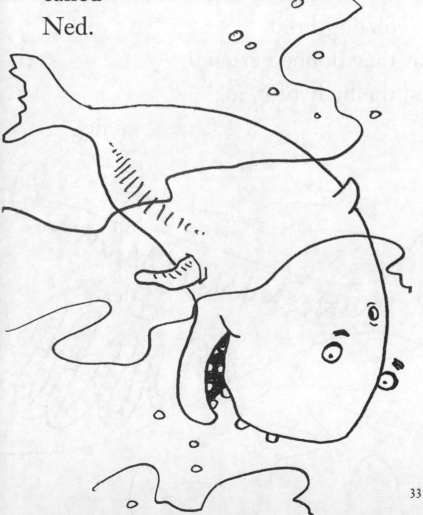

'Bother!' said Ed.
'Bother!' said Ted.
'Woof! Woof! Woof!' said
Ted's dog Fred,
as they bobbed around
in the belly of Ned.

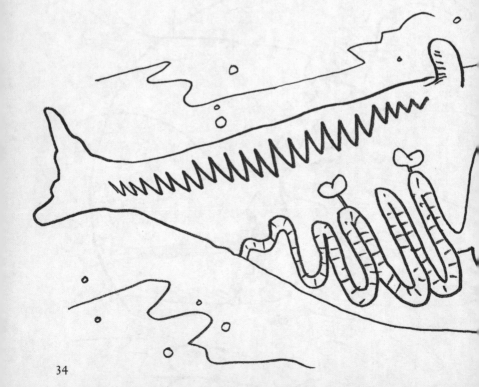

Ed and Ted and Ted's dog Fred
were certain
they were surely dead,
but the
whale called Ned—
who was overfed—

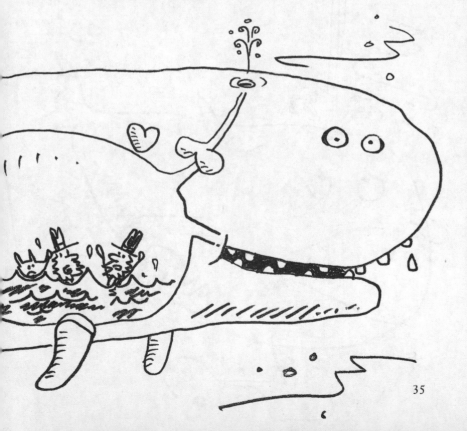

blew Ed
and Ted
and Ted's dog Fred
out of
the hole
in the top
of his head.

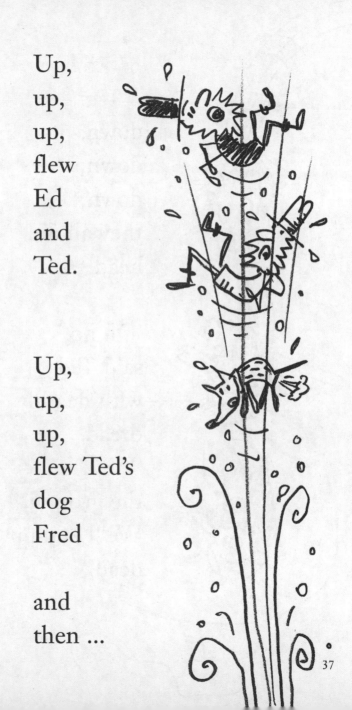

Up,
up,
up,
flew
Ed
and
Ted.

Up,
up,
up,
flew Ted's
dog
Fred

and
then ...

37

down,
down,
down,
they all did
head!

'Oh no,'
said Ted
with deathly
dread.
'We'll hit
the ground.
We'll end up
dead!'

'Fear not,'
said Ed,
to his friend Ted,
stretching a
handkerchief
over his head.
'Hang on to me, Ted!
Hang on to Ted, Fred!'
and
down
to
the
ground
they
para-chut-ed.

'Thank you,
        thank you, Ed!' said Ted.
'Thanks to you we are not dead!'
'Woof! Woof! Woof!'
said Ted's dog Fred
as he jumped up
and LICKED
Ed's head.

Ed
hugged
Fred!

Fred
hugged
Ed!

Ted
hugged
Fred!

Fred
hugged
Ted!

Ed
hugged
Ted!

Ted
hugged
Ed!

And
they
lived happily
ever after ...
in their shed.

PINKY PONKY THE SHONKY, WONKY, BONKY DONKEY

This is the story of Pinky Ponky.
Pinky Ponky was a donkey.

Tail

Pinky Ponky's tail was shonky.

Leg →

Pinky Ponky's leg was wonky.

Pinky Ponky's brain was bonky.

And that's the story
of Pinky Ponky:
the shonky,
wonky,
bonky
donkey.

FROG
ON A
LOG
IN A
BOG

There once was a frog
who lived in a bog.

The frog rode around
on a jet-rocket log.
There was no faster
frog in the bog.

But then one day
while riding its log
the frog looked up
and saw a dog.
The dog
was riding
a jet-rocket cog.

'My cog is faster
than your boggy old log,'
said the dog on a cog
to the frog on a log.

'My log is faster
than your rusty old cog,'
said the frog on a log
to the dog on a cog.

'We'll see about that!'
said the dog on a cog.
'I challenge you, frog,
to a race round the bog!'

'I agree!' said the frog.
'It's you and your cog
versus me and my log ...

and I'm going
to beat you,
Dog-on-a-cog.'

But just then
along came
the boss
of the bog:
a big fat hairy
slob of a hog.

'STOP!' said the hog
to the dog and the frog.
'Racing is NOT
allowed in my bog!
Not on a log!
Not on a cog!
No log-racing frogs!
No cog-racing dogs!
Do you hear me,
Frog-on-a-log?
Do you hear me,
Dog-on-a-cog?'

But the dog and the frog
just laughed at the hog—

and took off at high speed
around the bog.

The frog on a log
got in front of the dog!

Then the dog on a cog
got in front of the frog!

The frog raced its log
and the dog raced its cog
around
and around
and around the bog

until ...

up ahead
they saw the hog
standing on top of a
wall made of logs!

'Stop!' cried the hog.
'Stop, dog!
Stop, frog!
Stop this race around my bog!'

'But we're going too fast!'
cried the frog on a log.
'We CANNOT stop!'
cried the dog on a cog.

Crash! Bang! Pow!

Kersplog!

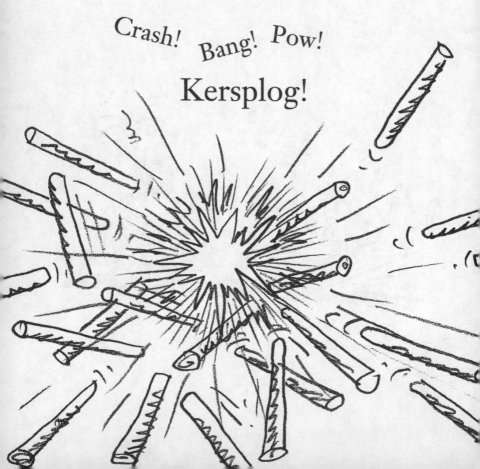

Into the air flew the dog and the frog.
Into the air flew the log and the cog.
Into the air flew the hog and his logs.

And then
down came the dog
on top of the cog!

Down came the frog
on top of the dog!

And last of all
down came the hog—
right on top of
the frog's
rocket log!

'Hey, this is fun!'
said the log-riding hog
as he rode the frog's log
past the dog and the frog.

'I'm the fastest hog on a log in the bog!
Try to catch me, dog and frog!
Try to catch me on the cog!'

'Okay!' said the frog.
'It's you on the log
versus us on the cog,
and we're going
to beat you,
Hog-on-a-log.'

And so the dog and the frog
on the jet-rocket cog
spent the rest of the day
racing the hog ...

around
and around
and around the bog.

HARRY BLACK, THE SACK, THE SNACK AND A SNEAKY SNACK-STEALING YAK CALLED JACK

There was a man
            called Harry Black.
Harry Black had a sack.
In his sack he had a snack.
He carried the sack
with the snack on his back.

One day while walking
down a track,
Harry Black met Jack the Yak.
'Hello, Jack,' said Harry Black.

'Hello, Harry Black,' said Jack.
'Is that a snack I can
smell in your sack?'

'Why, yes, it is,'
    said Harry Black.
'I carry a snack
in the sack on my back.'

'Can I have some, Harry Black?'
said Jack the Yak, who had no snack.

'No way, Jack,' said Harry Black.
'Get your own snack, Jack the Yak!'

'You'll be sorry,'
said Jack the Yak.
'You'll be sorry, Harry Black!'

But Harry Black
just turned his back
and kept on walking
down the track
until he saw
a big haystack.

'I think I'll have a little nap
and rest my sore and aching back,'
said the very tired Harry Black,
as he climbed the haystack
with his sack.

But while Harry Black
enjoyed his nap,
Jack the Yak
snuck into the sack
and ate up all of Harry's snack.

Then Jack the sleepy,
snack-filled Yak
fell fast asleep
in Harry's sack.

'Alas! Alack!' cried Harry Black
when he woke up—
opened his sack—
and found Jack the Yak
in place of his snack.

'Alas! Alack! What a setback!
My snack has been stolen
by a snack-stealing yak!'
said the very angry Harry Black.
'I'm going to give that yak a whack!'

But Jack the Yak
jumped out of the sack
and yelled, 'Get back,
I've got a tack!
And it's a SHARP one,
Harry Black!'

'Alas! Alack!' said Harry Black.
'I cannot give that yak a whack!
Or he'll attack me with that tack!'

And then Jack the Yak
with his sharp tack
jumped out of the sack
and fled on horseback.

So …

if you're ever walking
down a track
carrying a snack in a sack
on your back
and you meet a snackless yak
called Jack,
don't hold back:
open your sack
and share your snack—

for Jack the sneaky,
snack-stealing Yak
might just have
a very sharp tack
and you could end up
like poor Harry Black—
alone and hungry
on a haystack
with nothing but
a snackless sack.

DUCK
IN A
TRUCK
IN THE
MUCK

There was a duck.
His name was Chuck.
Chuck the Duck
drove an ice-cream truck.

But one wet day Chuck's
truck got stuck.

'What bad luck,'
said Chuck the Duck.
'My ice-cream truck
is stuck in muck.'

But just then
along came
his friend Buck
in his brand-new
shiny
muck-sucking
truck!

'Hey, Buck,' said Chuck,
'my truck is stuck. My truck is stuck
in all this muck.'

'You're in luck, Chuck,'
said Buck the Duck.
'I can get your truck unstuck.

I can suck up all the muck
with the muck-sucker-upper
on my muck-sucking truck!'

'Thank you, thank you, Buck,'
said Chuck.
'What are friends for?'
said Buck to Chuck.

Buck's
muck-sucker-upper
began to suck.

It sucked
and sucked
and sucked
and sucked
until all the muck
had been
sucked up.

'Hooray!' cried Chuck
as he ran to his truck.

'Get back, Chuck!'
yelled Buck the Duck.
'I haven't yet shut my muck-sucker up.'

But it was too late
        for Chuck the Duck—
he got sucked up into the truck.

And then the muck-sucker
sucked up Buck!

The muck-sucker-upper just
kept on sucking.

It sucked
and sucked
and sucked
and sucked ...

until Buck the Duck's
brand-new truck
got too full and
it
blew
up!

Out flew Chuck.

Out flew Buck.

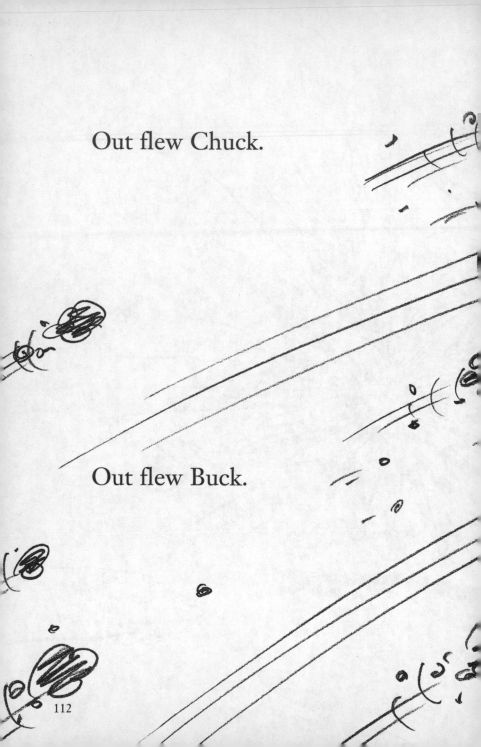

Out flew all the sucked-up muck.

'Boo-hoo,' cried Buck.
'My brand-new truck!
My brand-new shiny
truck blew up!'

'Don't cry, Buck,'
said the kind duck Chuck.
'We can share my
ice-cream truck!'

'Do you mean it, Chuck?'
said Buck.
'What are friends for?'
said Chuck to Buck.

So Buck hopped up
with Chuck the Duck
and they drove off together
in their ice-cream truck.

UNLUCKY LOU,
A KIND KANGAROO,
A HOLE IN A SHOE
AND SOME
EXTRA-SUPER-FAST-
STICKING
SUPER-ROO-GLUE

There once was a girl
called
Unlucky Lou:
the unluckiest girl
that the world
ever knew.

One day while visiting
at the zoo,
Lou found a hole
in the sole
of her shoc.

'Boo-hoo!'
cried Lou,
'what
will
I do?
If only
I had
some
Superglue!'

'Don't cry, Lou,'
said a kind kangaroo.
'You can borrow
some of my
super-roo-glue!
It's even more super
than Superglue
AND it's extra-super-fast-sticking too!'

'Oh, thank you, thank you!'
said Lou to the roo.
'Thanks to you
and your super-roo-glue
now I can fix
the hole in my shoe.'

But while super-roo-gluing
the hole in her shoe,
Lou slipped and spilt
almost all of the glue,
and then she tripped
and fell in it, too.

'Boo-hoo!' cried Lou,
'now what
will I
do?

I've fixed the hole
in the sole
of my shoe,
but now I'm stuck
in all this goo!'

But the kangaroo
knew just what to do.

It jumped over the fence
and kicked poor Lou,
as hard as only a roo can do.

Out of the glue
flew Unlucky Lou.
Up into the air
she flew and flew!

She flew right over
the walls of the zoo

and landed head-first
where a prickle-bush grew.

Poor old prickle-headed
Superglued Lou:

the unluckiest girl
that the world ever knew!

BILL
AND PHIL
AND
THE
VERY
BIG HILL

There was a man.
His name was Bill.
Bill had a friend.
His name was Phil.

One day Bill and his friend Phil
climbed to the top of a very big hill.

'I dare you to roll
down the hill,'
said Bill.

'I will if you will, Bill,'
said Phil.
'I will if you will, Phil,'
said Bill.

So Bill and Phil
rolled down the hill.

Faster and faster
rolled Phil and Bill.

'Help!' said Bill.
'I'm feeling ill!'
'Me too,' said Phil.
'It's a VERY big hill!'

But Bill and Phil
kept rolling until
they landed in a puddle of

smelly pig swill!

'Yuck!' said Bill.
'Yuck!' said Phil.

'Do you want to do it again?' said Bill.
'I will if you will, Bill,' said Phil.
'I will if you will, Phil,' said Bill.

So ...

once more they climbed
that very big hill
and rolled back down
into the swill.

And then they did it again ...

and again ...

and again …

and for all I know
they're doing it still.

ANDY G,
TERRY D,
THE BRAVE TEA-LADY
AND
THE EVIL BEE

One day while out walking
by the sea,
I saw a sign saying,
'BEWARE OF THE BEE.
YOU'LL GET STUNG
UNLESS YOU FLEE!'

But before I could flee,
I saw the bee.
And, even worse,
that bee saw me.

I had to run.
I had to flee.
As fast as my feet
could carry me.

As I ran I saw Terry D
and he looked up and he saw me.
'Why do you run so fast?' said he.
'Where are you going, Andy G?'

'The bee!' I cried.
'Can't you see?
That evil bee is after me.
From that bee I must flee
or it will surely bee-sting me.'

'I see, I see,' said Terry D.
'I see the bee.
I see that I must also flee.
I'll come with you, Andy G.'

And so Terry D ran after me.

We ran and ran quite speedily.
We passed a lady selling tea.
'Why are you running
so fast?' said she.
'Won't you stop and have some tea?'

'No time for tea,' said Terry D.
'We're being chased by an evil bee.
From that bee we must flee
or stung by the bee
we'll surely be.'

'I see,' said the lady selling tea.
'I see the bee.
I see that I must also flee.
Jump aboard my trolley with me.
It's a super-fast trolley
that is powered by tea.'

And so we fled.
We fled, all three.
As fast as we could—
pursued by that bee.

But just as we were almost free
the tea-trolley crashed
into a mighty tree.
'Quick!' said Terry,
'climb up the tree.
As fast as you can,
because here
comes the bee.'

Up we climbed.
One, two, three!
Terry D, the tea-lady and me.
We climbed and climbed
and climbed, we three.

We climbed right up
to the top
of that tree
until there was
nowhere left to flee.

I turned to face our enemy—
that evil, nasty, stinging bee—
and said to it most angrily,
'Why do you seek
to sting us three?
Just buzz off and let us be.'

But the bee just buzzed
with evil glee
and made a bee-line
straight for me!

But I didn't get stung
by that evil bee
thanks to the tea-lady's bravery.
She quickly jumped
in front of me
and waved her teapot
threateningly.
'STOP!' she cried,
'you nasty bee!'

But STOP
that nasty bee
DID NOT …

and so she
trapped it in her pot!

'Yippee! Yippee!' cried Terry D.
'No longer will that bee fly free.'

'Now,' sighed
the tea-lady
cheerfully,
'how about
that cup of tea?'

So we all sat down
at the top of the tree
and shared a pot
of fresh bee tea.

WHAT BUMOSAUR IS THAT?

An illustrated guide to prehistoric bumosaurs

By Andy Griffiths and Terry Denton

Professional bumosaurologists Andy Griffiths and Terry Denton have created a fully illustrated guide to assist the speedy and accurate identification of bumosaurs and bumosaur related life forms.

Covering all major bumosaurs from the Pre-crappian era through to the Post Crapaceous, this book includes startling full page illustrations of Common Bumosaurs, Great Big Bumosaurs, Sewersaurs, Bumosaurs of the Air, Horriblosaurs, Freakasaurs, Prehistoric Bumfish, Deep Water Bumosaurs, Disgustosaurs and Craposaurs.

Impress your friends! Amaze your family! Never again will you need to look like a fool when somebody asks you: 'What Bumosaur is that?'!

THE BAD BOOK
By Andy Griffiths
Illustrated by Terry Denton

In a bad, bad wood,
There was a bad, bad house.

And in that bad, bad house,
There was a bad, bad room.

And in that bad, bad room,
There was a bad, bad cupboard.

And in that bad, bad cupboard,
There was a bad, bad shelf.

And on that bad, bad shelf,
There was a bad, bad box.

And in that bad, bad box,
There was a BAD, BAD book ...

AND THIS IS IT!

JUST DISGUSTING!

By Andy Griffiths

Illustrated by Terry Denton

Is this the right book for you?
Take the DISGUSTING TEST and find out.

YES NO

☐ ☐ Do you ever pick your nose?
☐ ☐ Do you ever pick other people's noses?
☐ ☐ Do you ever find unidentified brown blobs in your bath?
☐ ☐ Do you think being able to burp the alphabet is an important life skill?
☐ ☐ Do you like stories about disgusting things like dead flies, giant slugs, maggots and brussel sprouts?

SCORE: One point for each 'yes' answer.
3-5 You are completely and utterly disgusting.
       You will love this book.
1-2 You are fairly disgusting.
       You will love this book.
0   You are either a liar or an adult (or both).
       You will love this book.

JUST CRAZY!

By Andy Griffiths

Illustrated by Terry Denton

Is this the right book for you?
Take the CRAZY TEST and find out.

YES NO

☐ ☐ Do you ever bounce so high on your bed that you hit your head on the ceiling?

☐ ☐ Do you ever look in the mirror and see a crazy maniac staring back at you?

☐ ☐ Do you like to read stories about kittens, puppies and ponies getting mashed and pulverised?

☐ ☐ Do you sometimes get the urge to take your clothes off and cover yourself in mud?

☐ ☐ Do you often waste your time taking crazy tests like this one?

SCORE: One point for every 'yes' answer.

3-5   You are completely crazy. You will love this book.

1-2   You are not completely crazy, but you're not far off it. You will love this book.

0   You are so far crazy you don't even realise you're crazy. You will love this book.

JUST STUPID!

By Andy Griffiths
Illustrated by Terry Denton

Is this the right book for you?
Take the STUPID TEST and find out.

YES NO

☐ ☐ Do you worry about getting sucked into the top of escalators?

☐ ☐ Do you push doors marked PULL and pull doors marked PUSH?

☐ ☐ Do you believe the bogeyman hides under your bed?

☐ ☐ Do you automatically turn around when somebody calls 'Hey, Stupid!'?

☐ ☐ Do you think that being able to stuff your mouth full of marshmallows is a sign of superior intelligence?

SCORE: One point for each 'yes' answer.

3-5 You are extremely stupid. You will love this book.

1-2 You are fairly stupid. You will love this book.

0 You think you're really smart but deep down you're as stupid as the rest of us.
   You will love this book.

JUST ANNOYING!

By Andy Griffiths

Illustrated by Terry Denton

Is this the right book for you?
Take the ANNOYING TEST and find out.

YES NO

☐ ☐ Do you ask 'Are we there yet?' over and over on long car trips?

☐ ☐ Do you like to drive people mad by copying everything they say and do?

☐ ☐ Do you hog the shower and use up all the hot water?

☐ ☐ Do you enjoy asking silly questions that have no real answers?

☐ ☐ Do you swing on the clothesline whenever you get the chance?

SCORE: One point for each 'yes' answer.

3-5 You are obviously a very annoying person.
     You will love this book.

1-2 You are a fairly annoying person.
     You will love this book.

0   You don't realise how much fun being annoying can be. You will love this book.

JUST TRICKING!
By Andy Griffiths
Illustrated by Terry Denton

Is this the right book for you?
Take the TRICKING TEST and find out.

YES NO

☐ ☐ Do you ever pretend that you are dead to get out of going to school?

☐ ☐ Do you like to ring people you know and pretend to be someone else?

☐ ☐ Do you leave banana skins in the middle of busy footpaths?

☐ ☐ Do you own any of the following items: fake dog poo, rubber vomit, gorilla suit?

☐ ☐ Do you wish that every day could be April Fools' Day?

SCORE: One point for each 'yes' answer.

3-5 You are a practical joking genius.
You will love this book.

1-2 You are a good practical joker.
You will love this book.

0 You are not a practical joker. You are what practical jokers call a 'victim'. You will love this book.